Bubble Bath PIRATES!

Jarrett J. Krosoczka

VIKING

VIKING
Published by the Penguin Group
Penguin Putnam Books for Young Readers, 345 Hudson Street, New York, New York 10014, U.S.A.
Penguin Books Ltd, 80 Strand, London WC2R 0RL, England
Penguin Books Australia Ltd, 250 Camberwell Road, Camberwell, Victoria 3124, Australia
Penguin Books Canada Ltd, 10 Alcorn Avenue, Toronto, Ontario, Canada M4V 3B2
Penguin Books (N.Z.) Ltd, 182-190 Wairau Road, Auckland 10, New Zealand

Penguin Books Ltd, Registered Offices: Harmondsworth, Middlesex, England

First published in 2003 by Viking, a division of Penguin Putnam Books for Young Readers.

3 5 7 9 10 8 6 4 2

LIBRARY OF CONGRESS CATALOGING-IN-PUBLICATION DATA
Krosoczka, Jarrett.
Bubble bath pirates / Jarrett J. Krosoczka.
p. cm.
Summary: When pirate mommy announces bath time, it is yo ho ho and
to the bath we go for her little pirates.
ISBN 0-670-03599-8
[1. Baths—Fiction. 2. Pirates—Fiction.] I. Title.
PZ7.K935 Bu 2003
[E]—dc21 2002008214

Manufactured in China
Set in Cafeteria and Blue Century
Book design by Kelley McIntyre

For
Michael, Brittany,
Matthew, and Griffin

"Yo ho, yo ho, it's off to

the bath we go!"

"All hands on deck!"
say her little pirates.

"Walk the plank!" commands the pirate mommy.

"Aye, aye matey,"
say her little pirates.

"Here's your washcloth,"
says the pirate mommy.

"Raise the sails!"
command her little pirates.

"Don't forget to scrub under your arms," pleads the pirate mommy.

"AHOY! Our arms be ticklish!"
giggle her little pirates.

"Close your eyes," warns the pirate mommy.

"Make sure you scrub your back,"
says the pirate mommy.

"Shiver me timbers!"
say her little pirates.

"Bath time is over,"
says the pirate mommy.

"prepare the cannons!"

yell her little pirates.

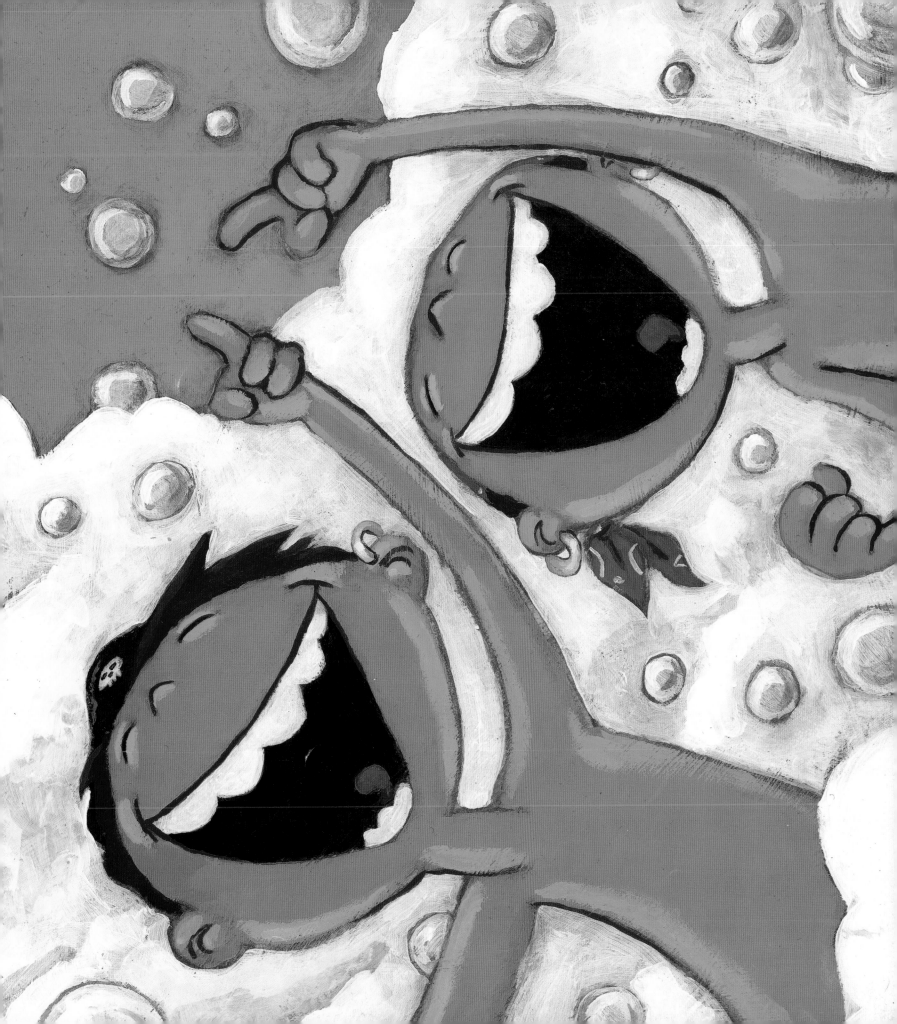

"OK, now who wants buried treasure in the kitchen?" asks the pirate mommy.

"GANGWAY!"
yell her little pirates.

now so sparkling clean."